5 MINUTE
Bedtime Tales

bookoli

Published in 2020 by Bookoli,
12 Laura Place, Bath BA2 4BL.
Bookoli is an imprint of Curious Universe UK Ltd.
Copyright © 2020 Curious Universe UK Ltd.
www.curiousuniverse.co.uk
Printed in China.

CONTENTS

Under the Sleepy Sky

The magic begins when the sun turns to gold,
Little ones yawn, bedtime stories are told.
A bath, a cuddle, a sweet lullaby,
Time to rest under the big, sleepy sky.

Rabbits twitch whiskers then homewards hop,
Birds seek a nest in the rustling treetop.
Donkeys lie down in cozy, straw beds,
Even the sheep become sleepyheads.

All over the world creatures curl up together,
Paw next to paw, and feather to feather.
Elephant, tiger cub, hippo and bee,
Mountain and farmyard, forest and sea.

Up in the north, reindeer huddle in tight,
Polar bears snuffle and snore through the night.

Down in the south, where it's steamy and hot,
Monkeys and meerkats snooze on the spot.

Sparkly stars twinkle high up above,
Mamas and babies with hearts full of love.
Kisses on noses, tucking up tails,
Bedtime for llamas, for otters, for whales.

There's quiet in the valley, the river and park.
But wait ... who is that peeping out of the dark?
Fox, cat and bat want to romp, roam and play,
Night-time is just the start of their day!

Dragon Camp

The bus rumbled up the road to the top of the mountain. Twelve little dragons sat inside, their faces pressed up to the window.

"Here we are, children," said the camp leader. "Smoulder Rock!

"WOW," shouted Lenny and Spike. **"SMOULDER ROCK!"**

Lenny and Spike were the loudest dragons on the bus. They were very excited.

WELCOME TO
SMOULDER
ROCK

"This is so awesome!" cried Lenny, pointing at the flagpole.

It was Lenny and Spike's very first Dragon Camp. Ever since they hatched out of their eggs, they had dreamed of being big enough to stay in a tent with their friends. They were finally here.

Dragon Camp was not as good as they had hoped it would be, **it was even better!**

After the little dragons put away their backpacks, the fun and games began.

They all built dens,

made fires and

played catch-the-dragon.

When it was dinnertime, the camp leader
banged his tail on the ground three times.

Gather around
the fire, please!

Bang!
Bang!
Bang!

Everyone sat in a big circle, gobbled down
a campfire supper and sang songs.

All around the mountain, the sky got darker
and darker.

"Time for bed now," said the camp leader.
Lenny leapt up. "BED? But I'm not ready!"

"Let's stay up all night!" whispered Spike.

13

The other dragons climbed into their sleeping bags and closed their eyes.

But Lenny and Spike had other ideas.

They did NOT want to sleep.

"How can we sleep when this bed is so bouncy?" asked Lenny, jumping up and down.

"How can we sleep when the stars are out?" asked Spike, getting out of his tent.

Go to sleep, Spike!

"How can I sleep when we can have midnight snacks?" giggled Lenny.
The other little dragons turned over and went to sleep.
But Lenny and Spike played all night long.

Early the next morning, the camp leader banged his tail on the ground three times.

"Good morning, little dragons!"

Ten little dragons helped raise the flag. Ten little dragons ate breakfast. The camp leader checked his list.

"Where are Lenny and Spike?" he asked.

The little dragons looked all around. And then they heard a noise from inside one of the tents...

Ten in the Bed

This is Poppy mouse.
Poppy lives in a tiny mouse house.

But Poppy isn't the only mouse living
in her tiny mouse house.

If you could peep inside Poppy's house, you would see mice chatting in the hallway, mice nibbling in the pantry and mice playing chase round the sofa.

Poppy is a small mouse with a

very BIG family.

Poppy's tiny mouse house is full of mice. Brothers and sisters, aunties and uncles, and too many cousins to count. And what a busy place it is! There are games and giggles all day long. Poppy never gets fed up.

Until it is time for bed.

In a tiny mouse house, everyone has to share. At night, Poppy snuggles up next to her mama and daddy, her brothers and sisters, and her dear old granny and grampy.

Ten mice in one little bed. Imagine that!
There is lots of fidgeting and fussing, wriggling
and rolling, sneezing and snoring.

One morning, Poppy had had enough.

"I need a bed of my own!" she decided.

Poppy jumped out of bed and scampered towards the door. "I don't want to share anymore," she whispered. "Bye bye, mouse house."

Poppy had never been away from home before. As she scuttled out onto the lane, it felt strange and exciting to be exploring on her own.

She soon spotted a beautiful bird swooping through the sky.

"Hello!" Poppy squeaked. "Do you have a comfy bed I could borrow?"

"Not me! I rest in a nest,"
called the bird, flying out of sight.

Poppy sighed. A nest was much too high
for a mouse to climb into.

Poppy walked on and on. She met different animals
along the way. Each time, she asked if they had
a bed she could borrow.

There was a horse that slept
in a stable (too chilly)...

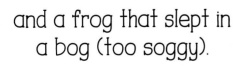

a mole that slept in a
hole (too creepy)...

and a frog that slept in
a bog (too soggy).

'Hmm. Maybe I can just make my own bed,' thought Poppy.

So she gathered up some hay
from the stable and some twigs and
leaves from the forest. Soon Poppy
had a cozy little home all of her own.

But it didn't feel quite right.
It was quiet. And cold.

Poppy felt strange.

As the sun started to set and
the forest turned dark,
she suddenly knew exactly where
she wanted to sleep.

"Sorry I'm late," yawned Poppy, scuttling back into her tiny mouse house. The candles were flickering, the mice were chatting and Poppy jumped onto the warm, cozy bed.

"There you are," said her daddy, lifting up the bed covers. "We are so happy to have you back home, little Pops."

Poppy climbed into bed. Ten little mice kissed her goodnight. Ten little mice snuggled her tight.

"Hmm," she sighed happily. "It's nice to explore but being at home is best. Maybe ten in the bed isn't so bad after all..."

Secret Island

Haven't you heard? Dog, Hare and Bird,
Took out their old wooden boat.

Off out to sea, happy friends three,
An afternoon spent all afloat.

The saltwater lapped,
all the friends napped,
The company easy and slow.
Then Bird flapped a wing,
and started to sing,

**"An island! Look there!
Shall we go?"**

Hare said, "Why, of course. We surely must visit."
Dog paddled the boat with his oar.
Then a mermaid so fair, with pearly-pink hair,
Waved to the friends from the shore.

What wonder was this? Something too good to miss,
With magic and spells everywhere.
Three friends afloat, in an old wooden boat,
Sang with the sounds in the air.

A fairy flew down and asked the friends three,
To come and join in with the fun.
As a unicorn show, lined up in a row,
The friends played and danced in the sun.

An island enchanted, a special dream granted,
But now their exploring was done.
Bird, Dog and Hare, breathed in the air,
And dropped off to sleep, one by one.

Haven't you heard? Dog, Hare and Bird,
Back in their old wooden boat.

Home from the sea, happy friends three,

An afternoon drifting afloat.

The Lost Roar

Kali was the roughest, toughest tiger in the jungle. She had sharp claws, pointy teeth and the loudest roar you ever did hear.

Every day after breakfast, Kali went on jungle patrol.

"Get out of my way!"

"Do as I say!"

"I'm queen today!"

Everyone was frightened of Kali. Even the other tigers didn't dare to get too close. She only had to roar, and they would run away.

"Ha!" she laughed, watching their stripy tails disappearing into the jungle. "That showed them!"

35

One day when Kali set off on jungle patrol,
she felt a strange tickle in her throat.

She prowled along the trail and she leapt
through the trees, just like usual. When she
got to the watering hole, she tried to scare
everyone off with a big, loud roar.

But there was silence. Kali blinked.
The animals stared.

"Atishoo!"

Instead of a roar, the queen of the jungle did
a big, noisy sneeze.

Nobody was scared. Nobody ran away. Kali had a cold!
The tiger turned on her tail and slunk back to her den.

Kali felt very sorry for herself indeed. Her throat was sore, her nose was blocked, but worst of all, the tiger had lost her roar.

"I can't be queen today," she grumbled. "I feel too poorly."

All over the jungle, the other tigers waited and listened. "Maybe Kali has left?" they said. "Perhaps she's gone to find a bigger, wilder jungle to rule."

The tigers grew more and more curious. One by one, they began to creep towards her jungle den.

"Where is she?"

they asked each other, padding right up to the entrance.

The tigers bravely went inside. "Look!" they whispered. Kali was there after all!

But Kali did not want to see the tigers.

"Please, just go away,' she rasped. Kali sunk back in shame. What use was a tiger without her roar?

The other tigers hurried away to talk. "What shall we do?" they asked. Even though Kali could be rough and tough, the tigers still wanted to help her.

"I'll fetch some soft, green leaves," said one tiger.

"I'll pick a juicy melon," said another.

"I'll collect some ferns," said another.

"We won't go away," they all told Kali.
"And you can't make us."

And then the tigers got to work.

They used green leaves to make a soft, comfy bed.
They gave Kali sweet melon to ease her sore throat.
And they fanned her with ferns when the sun got too hot.

Kali purred in surprise. She was feeling better in no time!
She promised to never scare the tigers away again.

"I lost my roar for a little while," Kali smiled,
"but I found true friends forever!"

Bedtime Bear

The hour was late. The sky was inky-blue. It was past the time when little animals should all be fast asleep.

But Little Bear trembled in his bed. The den was dark. Outside, he could hear strange noises. He wished that the morning would hurry up and come around again.

"Mama," said Little Bear. **"Wake up, Mama!"**

"I'm here, Little Bear," she whispered. "Just like always."
"There are noises outside," said Little Bear. "It's so dark.
I don't like the night. It makes me feel afraid."

Mama scooped Little
Bear into her arms.
"Afraid?" she asked.
"You'd better come
with me…"

Mama carried Bear out of the den. She put him down beside her, underneath the old fir tree.

"Now look around you, Little Bear," she murmured.

"What do you see?"

Little Bear peeped out from behind his paws. The forest was dark. "Nothing! There's nothing to see!" he decided.

Mama pointed up to the sky. "Is that so?" she asked.

Bear gazed up above him. Slowly, very slowly, his eyes got used to the night. Thousands of stars twinkled overhead. He gasped in surprise.

"Oh Mama!" he whispered. "It's beautiful."

The night breeze swirled through the forest. Bear heard a rustle on the ground and a hoot up above. He jumped onto his mama's lap. "What was that, Mama?"

Mama smiled. "Keep looking and listening."

45

Bear sat quietly. He looked and he listened.

Owls swooped through the trees, eyes open wide as they sang their magical too-whit-too-woo.

Baby badgers danced in the glow of the moon, rustling and tumbling in the fallen leaves.

Little mice held secret midnight feasts, sharing berries and seeds with their friends.

"You see?" whispered Mama softly. "You are never alone, even when the sky is dark."

Bear looked all around. There was nothing to be afraid of.

Night-time was wonderful!

Sweet dreams, Little Bear.